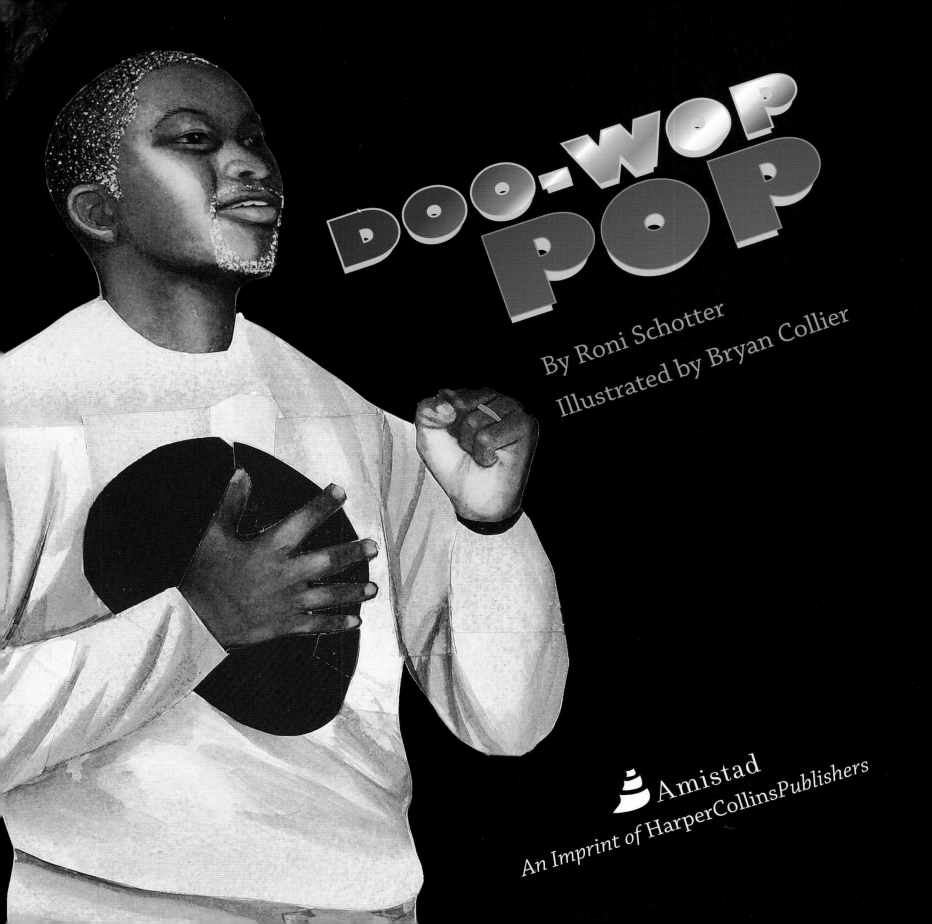

DOO-WOP POP

By Roni Schotter

Illustrated by Bryan Collier

Amistad
An Imprint of HarperCollinsPublishers

To Rick of the Hollywoods, Bop-Boppa-lock™ you rock.
—R.S.

Thanks to Mr. Ellis and the students of St. Mark's in Harlem,
New York, for allowing me to represent them in this book.
—B.C.

Amistad is an imprint of HarperCollins Publishers.

Doo-Wop Pop
Text copyright © 2008 by Roni Schotter
Illustrations copyright © 2008 by Bryan Collier

Manufactured in China.

www.harpercollinschildrens.com

Library of Congress Cataloging-in-Publication Data is available.
ISBN 978-0-06-057968-5 (trade bdg.) — ISBN 978-0-06-057974-6 (lib. bdg.)

Typography by Jeanne L. Hogle
1 2 3 4 5 6 7 8 9 10
❖
First Edition

Well, they used to call him Snow Man, but his real name is Mr. Searle. He's old but cool. He cleans our school—with a broom and a mop. And his sounds . . . he calls them doo-wop. In the "oldie-but-goodie" days, he was lead singer with the Icicles. He sang doo-wop— **"Sha-bop, sha-bop, my baby."** "Let me tell you," he says, "we were smooooooth! People stopped to hear us sing, watch us move."

Now when Doo-Wop Pop sweeps, I do my hide-and-peek. I like to watch him. He takes one step forward and goes **"sha-boom"** with his broom. He takes another step back and says **"sha-bop"** with his mop. **"Doo-woppa-dop,"** he adds with a hop. *That's* why we call him Doo-Wop Pop.

Me, they call the Slipper, but my real name's Elijah Earl. I won't lie . . . I'm shy. While other kids are talking, I keep on walking. I slip away. . . .

In our school I'm not alone. There are three or four like me—on their own. Under her head scarf, Alishah hides more than her hair. And Jacob? He twitches when the other kids stare. Luis likes to burrow his head in a book so no one can spot him or give him a look. Then . . . there's Pam Pam. She's even shyer than I am!

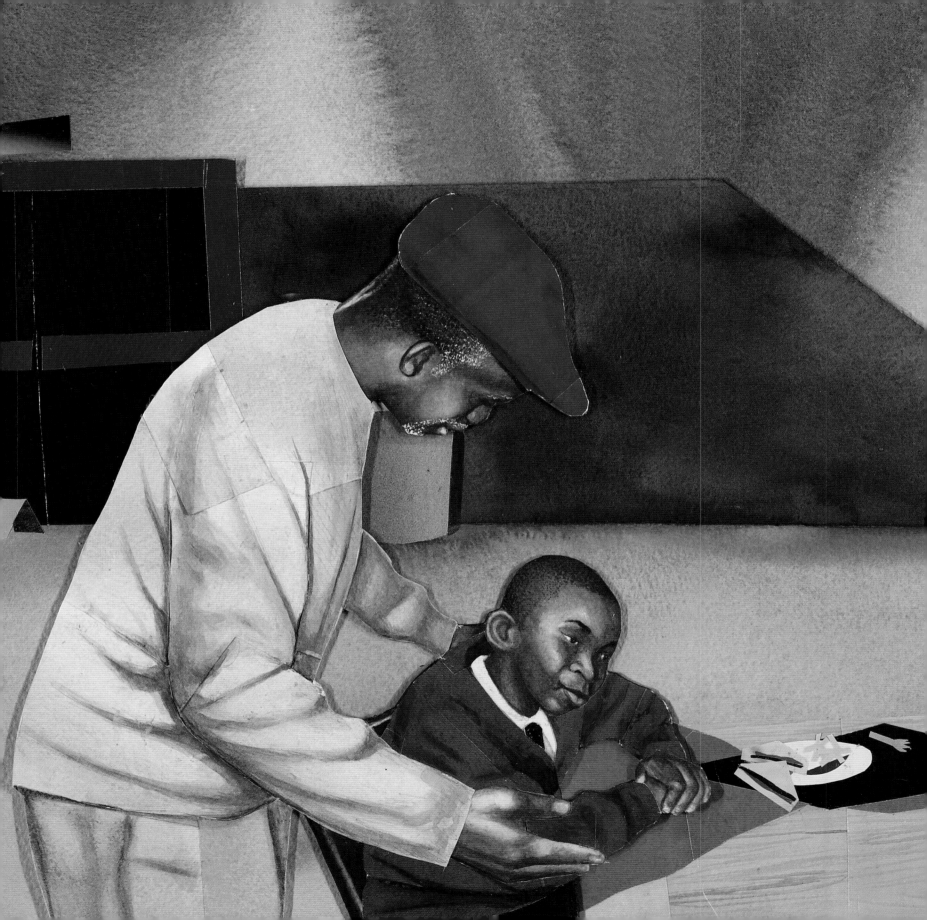

One day in the lunchroom, I'm sitting solo, eating my PB and J, when Doo-Wop Pop comes over, smiles, and says, "Hey."

"I see you," he says, "always hiding, taking your notes. So take this down—one of my favorite quotes: 'It's no disgrace to show your face.'"

I swallow some air, along with some fear. When I finally look up, his face is near. I'm inches from the diamond that shines in his ear.

"Not long ago, I was just like you—on the edge of the world, didn't know what to do. Man, I was *caught* . . . till one day, eating lunch, I thought, 'Stop being the carrot that stays out of the soup. Dive in with the potatoes. Be part of the group.'"

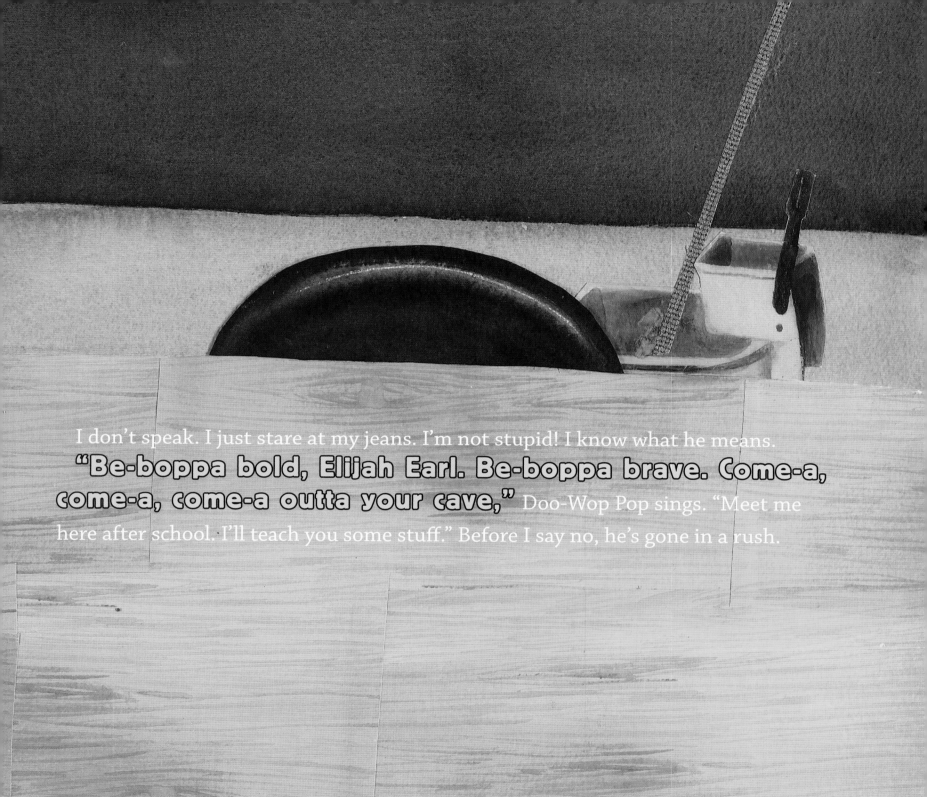

I don't speak. I just stare at my jeans. I'm not stupid! I know what he means. **"Be-boppa bold, Elijah Earl. Be-boppa brave. Come-a, come-a, come-a outta your cave,"** Doo-Wop Pop sings. "Meet me here after school. I'll teach you some stuff." Before I say no, he's gone in a rush.

At 3:10 school's out, and what can I say?
My butterflies are fluttering in a *really* bad
way. I'm asking myself should I go or stay
when, suddenly—

"Good! All my carrots are here. Dive in!
Watch my feet. Do what I do. Follow the
beat. Gonna teach you the moves. So . . .
step right. Step left. Cross over, now back.
Lean forward. Lean backward. Let your
fingers snap. Again!"

I try but can't do it. My feet are a twist.
I'm a pretzel, not a dancer. I know soon I'll
be dissed! But when I dare to take a peek at
the others and their feet, I see that they're
tangled, too. Everyone's doing the best they
can do.

"Sha-doo bop-a-lop," says Doo-Wop Pop. "You kids are the top! Now stop. All you need now is music—your own special song."

"But aren't you going to teach it to us," Luis asks softly, "so we can sing along?"

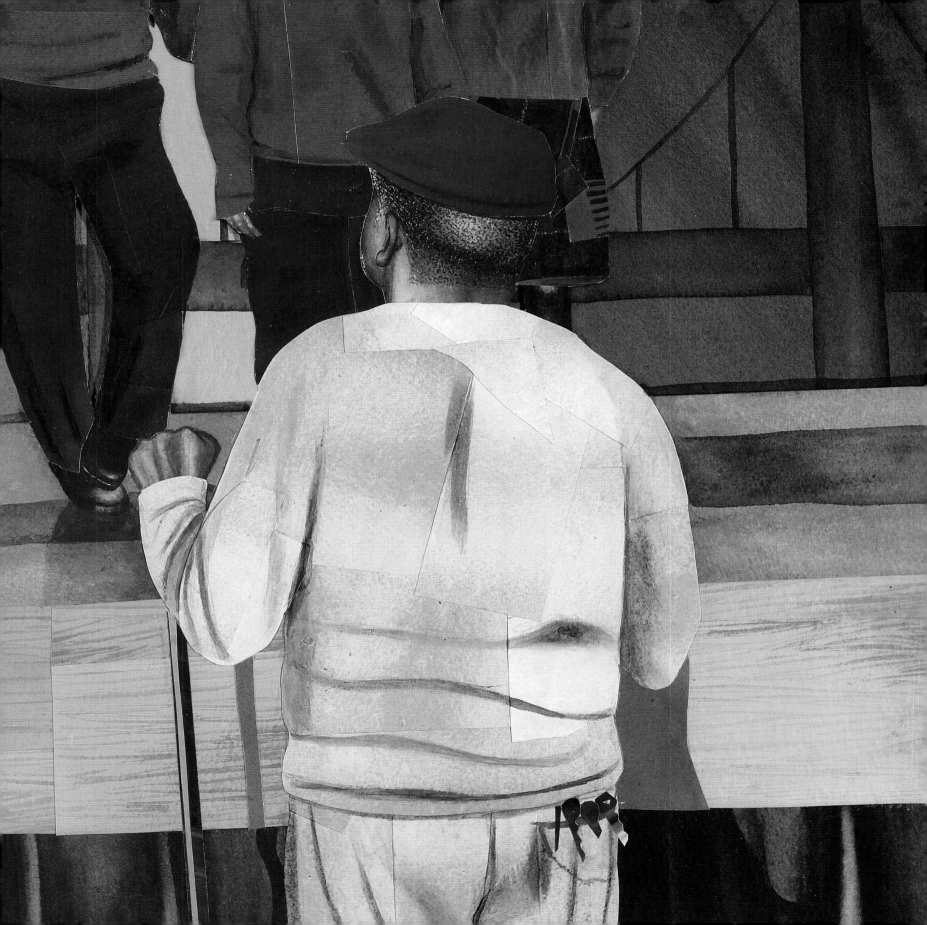

"Wrong. That's your job. Stop, look, and listen to the world. Catch the thing that makes you feel like you just have to sing! There's music in the air—inside, outside—everywhere. There's doo-wop, pop, bebop, hip-hop, rap, boogie-woogie, punk, funk, salsa, ska, jazz, and rock—even Mr. J. S. Bach—and *he's* one cool dude! As for words? They fly among us like beautiful birds."

"B-b-but," I say. "How can we? None of us, w-w-well, not even . . . a . . . one of us has an instrument to play."

"Wella, wella, wella, my doubting young fella." Doo-Wop Pop laughs. "That's why we call it *a cappella*."

And Doo-Wop Pop sits us down and tells us how he used to travel 'round singing doo-wop—with no instruments! He says he was quite the sight! He wore a suit so gleaming white, some folks said it was made of moonlight. He kept a handkerchief in his pocket in a diamond shape, and he wore a cape—lined with silver-speckled crepe! One night he got to sing on the stage of a place so great, and of such account, it was called the Paramount.

"All that was a long time ago, but one day," he says, "I know I'll sing again on a stage! You have to have a dream, especially at my age. For now I've got my today work to do, and now, my sweet carrots, so do you!" Then Doo-Wop Pop, he grabs his broom. With a slide and a spin, he leaves the room.

The very next day, we start to meet, and like Mr. Searle told us, we listen for the beat—for the music of our world—the **click-click-clack** of feet in the halls, the burst of laughter through the walls, the kids in the orchestra rehearsing onstage, the rattle of a turning page.

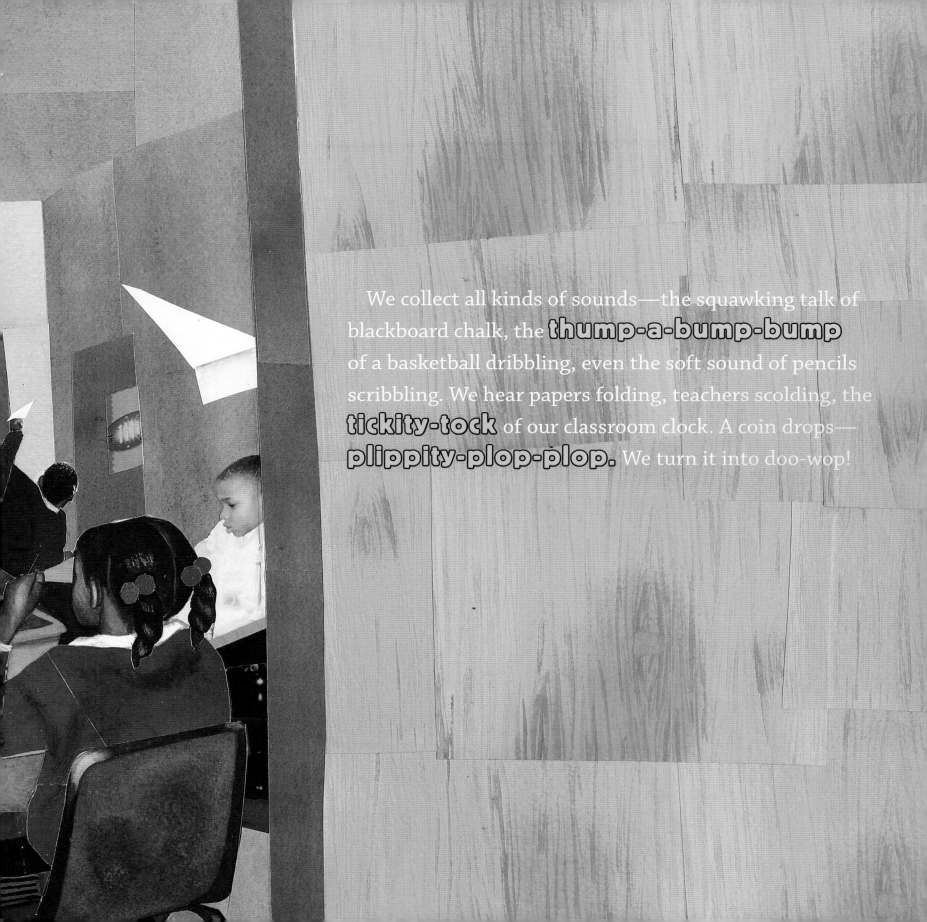

We collect all kinds of sounds—the squawking talk of blackboard chalk, the **thump-a-bump-bump** of a basketball dribbling, even the soft sound of pencils scribbling. We hear papers folding, teachers scolding, the **tickity-tock** of our classroom clock. A coin drops— **plippity-plop-plop.** We turn it into doo-wop!

When we start singing together, we discover a treat—Alishah has rhythm feet! She can **rappity-tap**—keep track of the beat. Luis sings high up, and when he lets go, he sings in what Mr. Searle calls *falsetto*.

Jacob? He's the best at singing bass. He sings so deep and low, there's nowhere lower he can go. As for Pam Pam? Well, she sure can **jam-jam!**

We practice each and every day, until one morning we hear Mr. Searle say, "You've been working a lot. Time to hear what you've got. Let's hear how you fare," and he opens the door that leads to the stair. "In the *stairwell*?" we ask. Steps, walls, tile? We don't buy it. "For the echo," Mr. Searle says. "Try it." "Okay," we say, but inside we're thinking, *No way!* But when the sound of our song bounces back off the tile, we sound soooo good, we start to smile! "*I knew you would!*" Mr. Searle says. We sing. We do our moves. Mr. Searle nods. He approves! I close my eyes. I hear the blend—each of us singing, each a new friend. One sings low. One sings sweet. When we sing together, we can't **be-boppa beat!**

I hear Mr. Searle clapping. He sounds awfully loud. I open my eyes. . . . Surprise! There's a crowd. The door's wide open. Everyone can hear us. Our principal, teachers, even the other kids cheer us! We blush. "Your fans," Mr. Searle says. "Just listen. . . ." His diamond eyes glisten. "My carrots—take a bow." We do and feel great.

WOW!

And now? **Wella, wella, wella,** this is how our story ends: The five of us? We've got new friends. **Ooby-dooby doop**—we're an even larger singing group! And Doo-Wop Pop? Well, he's put away his broom and mop. Every day now, after school, he *teaches* doo-wop. But the most amazing thing?

One night we climbed onstage to sing! Were we scared? You bet! But we told ourselves, **"Be-boppa brave. Be-boppa bold!"** And though our knees shook and our palms were cold, let me tell you—we carrots—how we rock-and-rolled!

PLATTERS

Cadillacs

Jewels

Heartbeats

Moonglows

Chantels

Teenagers

Penguins

DALLAS

Cadillacs

Belles

Teen Chor

Teen

STUDENTS

Skyliners

Valentines